Farmyard Tales

Rusty's Train Ride

Heather Amery

Adapted by Susanna Davidson

Illustrated by Stephen Cartwright

Reading consultant: Alison Kelly

Find the duck on every double page.

This story is about Apple Tree Farm,

Poppy,   Sam,

Mrs. Boot
the farmer,

Mrs. Hill,

Rusty,

Mopp
the puppy

and a steam train.

Poppy and Sam were
having breakfast.

"What are we doing today?" asked Sam.

"Let's go and see the steam train," said Mrs. Boot.

"Hooray!" said Poppy and Sam.

They walked down the hill to the station.

"Here comes the train!" cried Poppy.

Choo! Choo!

Mrs. Hill and her
puppy were at the
station too.

Everyone chatted with
the train driver.

Choo! Choo! Choo! The train was ready to go.

"Where's Mopp?" cried Mrs. Hill. "Where's my puppy?"

Rusty pulled and pulled
until Sam let go.

Then Rusty jumped
onto the train.

"Come back, Rusty!"
cried Sam.

Everyone shouted and waved. But the train didn't stop.

"We'll have to wait for it to come back," said Mrs. Boot.

At last, the train
chugged back.

"Look! There's Rusty,"
said Poppy.

"But where's my little Mopp?" asked Mrs. Hill.

Out came Rusty... with little Mopp!

"Thank you, Rusty,"
said Mrs. Hill.

"You looked after little
Mopp for me."

"Rusty and Mopp
went for a train ride,"
said Sam.

"Now can we go for one too?"

PUZZLES

Puzzle 1

Put these pictures in the right order to tell the story.

A.

B.

C.

D.

E.

Puzzle 2

Who's who? Match the names to the people or animals in this story.

Sam

Poppy

Mrs. Boot

Mrs. Hill

Mopp

Rusty

Puzzle 3

Can you spot five differences between these two pictures?

Puzzle 4

Choose the right sentence for each picture.

A.

It puffed out smoke.

It puffed out sausages.

B.

"Here's Mopp."

"Where's Mopp?"

C.

Then he jumped off the train!
Then he jumped onto the train!

D.

At last, the train came back.
At last, the bus came back.

Answers to puzzles

Puzzle 1

1B.

2D.

3A.

4E.

5C.

Puzzle 2

Poppy

Sam

Mrs. Hill

Mrs. Boot

Mopp

Rusty

Puzzle 3

Puzzle 4

A. It puffed out smoke.

B. "Where's Mopp?"

C. Then he jumped onto the train!

D. At last, the train came back.

Designed by Laura Nelson
Series editor: Lesley Sims
Series designer: Russell Punter
Digital manipulation by Nick Wakeford

This edition first published in 2016 by Usborne Publishing Ltd.,
Usborne House, 83-85 Saffron Hill, London EC1N 8RT, England.
www.usborne.com Copyright © 2016, 1999 Usborne Publishing Ltd.

USBORNE FIRST READING
Level Two

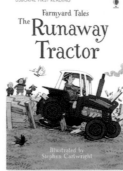

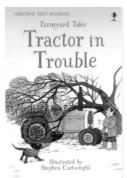

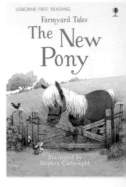

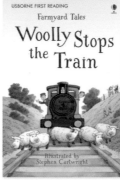

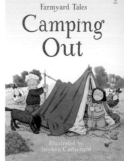